Richmond Punch Office

The Punch Songster

A Collection of Familiar and Original Songs and Ballads

Richmond Punch Office

The Punch Songster
A Collection of Familiar and Original Songs and Ballads

ISBN/EAN: 9783744786171

Printed in Europe, USA, Canada, Australia, Japan

Cover: Foto ©Andreas Hilbeck / pixelio.de

More available books at **www.hansebooks.com**

CONTENTS.

THE

PUNCH SONGSTER.

A COLLECTION OF

FAMILIAR AND ORIGINAL

SONGS AND BALLADS.

———— •••• ————

RICHMOND:
PUNCH OFFICE.
1864.

PREFACE.

We commit this collection of Songs and Ballads to the hands of our gallant soldiers in the field. It cannot enlarge their patriotic devotion to the best interests of their country—if, however, it tends to lesssen the tedium of camp-life, we are more than satisfied.

Many of the songs contained in this unpretending volume are original, and adapted to familiar airs.

JEM WELLS, OF THE NEW RICHMOND THEATRE.

COMIC SONGS.

THE CONSCRIPT'S LAMENT.

AS SUNG BY HENRY T. ALLEN AT THE NEW RICHMOND THEATRE.

I'll tell you, boys, in Richmond the times are getting tight,
For all young men who have no mind to go to the field and fight;
Some lay down their tens, and others hundreds more,
For a little piece of paper saying, "I'm from Baltimore."

I put in a substitute and thought I was all right,
But I found that I could not come it, that I had to go and fight;
I went before the Surgeon, and Dr. Early says,
"Well, you're a clever fellow, and I'll give you twenty days."

Then I tried the blockade, they told me that was sure,
I could get a man to put me through, that his name was Doc.
    McClure;
The pickets took me up, and they told me very polite,
That no one passes through the lines except an Israelite.

Then I tried the contract, and every way contrived,
But soon found out it wouldn't do, I was under forty-five;
The guards took me on the street, and call'd it a funny joke,
And took me up before a man, they call'd him Captain Coke.

Now Coke, he is a nice young man, so everybody says,
But he told me to report to camp with rations for three days;
Oh, dear! I am so tired, I don't know what to do,
I'd like to take a little nap and sleep a year or two.

Now I tell all you young men who have no wish to fight,
You had better take your naps by day and prowl around at night,
For the guards will pick you up, sure as two and two make four,
And they'll put you in the army till this "cruel war" is o'er.

THE MISS-NOMERS.

Miss Brown is exceedingly fair,
　Miss White is as red as a berry,
Miss black has a gray head of hair,
　Miss Graves is a flirt very merry;
Miss Lightbody weighs sixteen stone,
　Miss Rich can scarce muster a guinea,
Miss Hare wears a wig and has none,
　And Miss Solomon is a sad ninny.

Miss Wright is constantly wrong,
　Miss Tickle, alas! is not funny,
Miss Singer ne'er warbled a song,
　And, alas! Miss Cash has no money;
Miss Bateman would give all she's worth
　To purchase a man to her liking,
Miss Merry is shocked at all mirth,
　Miss Boxer the men don't find striking

Miss Mildmay's a terrible scold,
　Miss Dove's ever coarse and contrary,
Miss Young is now grown very old,
　And Miss Heavyside's light as a fairy;
Miss Short is at least five feet ten,
　Miss Noble's of humble extraction,
Miss Love has a hatred toward men,
　While Miss Still is forever in action

Miss Green is eternally blue,
　Miss Scarlet is pale as a lily,
Miss Violet never shrinks from our view,
　And Miss Wiseman thinks all men silly
Miss Goodchild's a naughty young elf,
　Miss Lion's from terror a fool,
Miss Mee's not at all like myself,
　Miss Carpenter no one can rule.

Miss Sadler ne'er mounted a horse,
　Miss Groom from the stable will run,
Miss Killmore can't look on a corse,
　And Miss Aimwell ne'er handled a gun;
Miss Greathead has no brains at all,
　Miss Hartwell is ever complaining,
Miss Dance ne'er has been at a ball, [ing.
　Over hearts Miss Fairweather likes reign-

Miss Bliss does with sorrow o'erflow,
  Miss Hope in despair seeks the tomb,
Miss Joy still anticipates woe,
  And Miss Charity's never "at home;"
Miss Hamlet resides in the city,
  The nerves of Miss Standfast are shaken
Miss Prettyman's beau is not pretty,
  Miss Faithful her love has forsaken.

Miss Porter despises all froth,   [ing,
  Miss Scales they'll make *wait* I am think-
Miss Meekly is apt to be wroth,
  Miss Lofty to meanness is sinking;
Miss Seymore's as blind as a bat,
  Miss Last at a party is first,
Miss Brindle dislikes a strip'd cat,
  And Miss Waters has always a thirst.

Miss Knight is now changed into day,
  Miss Day wants to marry a Knight,
Miss Prudence has just run away,
  And Miss Steady assisted her flight;
But, success to the fair, one and all,
  No mis-apprehensions be making;
Though wrong the dear sex to *mis*-call,
  There's no harm, I hope, in *mis*-taking.

LINCOLN'S DREAM.

Air—Cork leg.

In Harrisburg Old Abe lay down,
To soothe his spirits, rest his crown;
While all the people in the town,
Devoted, watched his dwelling round,
    Ri tu, di nu, ri tu, di nu,
    Ri tu, di nu, di na.

He dreamed an awful dream that night,
He saw a sad and fearful sight,
His hair on end stood with affright,
His "Jackson" nerves were shaken quite.
    Ri tu, di nu, &c.

Havre de Gras and Baltimore,
Plug Uglies, Blood Tubs, twenty score,
Came forth to taste of human gore,
An awful, rampant, vengeful corps.
    Ri tu, di nu, &c.

He turned to Mrs. Lincoln then,
This President, yet pig of men,
"My dear," said he, "I see them all,
Each bloody, thugging cannibal."
    Ri tu, di nu, &c.

"How do they flourish?" then said she,
"If I were a man, they couldn't scare me
Face them, and down with the reckless
        crew."
"*You* may!" said he— "d—d if *I* do!"
    Ri tu, di nu, &c.

So he muffled up in a Scottish plaid,
And a regimental coat, 'tis said—
Cut out on the cars, with fright half dead,
And left Mrs. L. snoring in bed.
    Ri tu, di nu, &c.

A patent safe he wanted sore,
When passing at night through Baltimore,
But safe was he disguised, and lone,
For the devil wouldn't know his own.
    Ri tu, di nu, &c.

And when arose the morning sun,
Over the spires of Washington,
All the town then rubbed their eyes,
In wonder, surmise and surprise.
    Ri tu, di nu, &c.

"Coward!" cried the Southrons then,
"Fool!" said Premier Seward's men;
"Come, to our arms!" the radicals cried,
"There's plenty of fat in that lean hide!"
    Ri tu, di nu, &c.

THE PERPLEXED HOUSEKEEPER.

I wish I had a dozen pairs
  Of hands this very minute;
I'd soon put all these things to rights—
  The very deuce is in it:

Here's a big washing to be done,
  One pair of hands to do it— [pants—
Sheets, shirts and stockings, coats and
  How will I e'er go through it?

Dinner to get for five or more,
  No loaf left o'er from Sunday,
And baby cross as he can live—
  He's always so on Monday.

And there's the cream, 'tis getting sour,
  And must forthwith be churning,
And here's Bob wants a button on—
  Which way shall I be turning?

'Tis time the meat was in the pot,,
   The bread was worked for baking
The clothes were taken from the boil—
   Oh dear, the baby's waking.

Hush, baby dear! there, hush, hush!
   I wish he'd sleep a little,
Till I could run and get some wood—
   To hurry up that kettle.

Oh dear, if P—— comes home
   And find things in this pother,
He'll just begin and tell me all
   About his tidy mother.

How nice *her* kitchen used to be,
   Her dinner always ready
Exactly when the noon-bell rung—
   Hush, hush, dear little Freddy.

And there will come some hasty word,
   Right out before I'm thinking—
They say that hasty words from wives
   Set sober men to drinking.

Now isn't that a great idea
   That men should take to sinning
Because a weary, half-sick wife
   Can't always smile so winning?

When I was young I used to earn
   My living without trouble,
Had clothes and pocket money, too,
   And hours of leisure double.

I never dreamed of such a fate,
   When I, *a lass!* was courted—
Wife, mother, nurse, seamstress, cook,
     housekeeper, chambermaid, laundress
     and scrub generally doing the work
     of six
For the sake of being supported.

PADDY O'RAFTHER.

Paddy, in want of a dinner one day,
Credit all gone, and no money to pay,
Stole from the priest a fat pullet, they say,
    And went to confession just afther;
" Your riv'rince," says Paddy, " I stole this fat hen."
" What, what!" says the priest, " at your old thricks again ?
Faith, you'd rather be stalin' than sayin' amen,
                    Paddy O'Rafther!"

" Sure you wouldn't be angry," says Pat, " if you knew
That the best of intintions I had in my view,
For I stole it to make it a prisint to you,
    And you can absolve me afther."
" Do you think," says the priest, " I'll partake of your theft ?
Of your seven small senses you must be bereft—
You're the biggest blackguard that I know, right or left,
                    Paddy O'Rafther!"

"Then what shall I do with the pullet," says Pat,
" If your riv'rince won't take it ? By this and by that
I don't know no more than a dog nor a cat
    What your riv'rince would have me be afther."
" Why then," says his riv'rince, " you sin-blinded owl,
Give back to the man that you stole from, his fowl,
For if you do not, 'twill be worse for your sowl,
                    Paddy O'Rafther."

Says Paddy, " I ask'd him to take it—'tis true
As this minit I'm talkin', your riv'rince, to you,
But he wouldn't resaive it—so what can I do ?"
    Says Paddy, nigh chokin' with laughter.
" By my throat," says the priest, " but the case is absthruse ;
If he won't take his hen, why the man is a goose—
'Tis not the first time my advice was no use,
                    Paddy O'Rafther."

But for sake of your sowl, I would sthrongly advise,
To some one in want you would give your supplies,
Some widow, or orphan, with tears in their eyes ;
    And then you may come to me, afther."

So Paddy went off to the brisk widow Hoy,
And the pullet, between them, was eaten with joy,
And, says she, "'Pon my word, you're the cleverest boy,
                                    Paddy O'Rafther."

Then Paddy went back to the priest, the next day,
And told him the fowl he had given away
To a poor lonely widow, in want and dismay,
    The loss of her spouse weeping afther.
"Well, now," says the priest, "I'll absolve you, my lad,
For repentantly making the best of the bad,
In feeding the hungry and cheering the sad,
                                    Paddy O'Rafther."

THOSE LOVELY FEET.

I saw her from my window
    Go tripping down the street;
Her form was most superb, but ah!
    Who ever saw such feet?

I heard them patter, patter go,
    Soft as an angel's tread;
"So small," said I, "I never saw
    Before, or even read."

I seized my hat and followed
    The unsuspecting fair,
And watched the lightly tripping feet,
    That seemed to tread on air.

Who can she be, I wondered;
    She's beautiful, I know—
A fairer woman never trod
    This earth of ours below!

She stopped—she dropped her 'kerchief
    (I am always quite gallant;)
I picked it up with prettiest bow,
    And thunder! 'twas my aunt!

MRS. CRINOLINE ABROAD.

Fluttering down the sidewalk,
  Flitting 'cross the street,
Head and hands in motion,
  Timing to her feet—
Right foot up and ready,
  Ere the left is down,
Bless me! what a bustle
  Coming through the town.

What a load of ribbons
  For one head to wear!
What a load of dry goods
  For one back to bear!
What a breadth of sidewalk
  For one skirt to hide!
How the little people
  Scatter on one side!

There is grandsire Toodle
  Coming down the street;
Poor old man—proud lady—
  Wonder how they'll meet!
Grandsire to a lamp-post
  Clings with vague surprise,
Madam cannot see him—
  Madam's lost her eyes.

Lookers-on are plenty,
  Jokes are very free;
Silly people wonder
  Much what she can be.
Man of science guesses,
  Looking very pale,
That it is a comet—
  Judging by the tail.

Farmer Dobbs conjectures,
  Winking both his eyes,
It is a walking haystack,
  By the shape and size;
It is a locomotive,
  Party third disputes,

Judging by the clatter
  Of the high-heel boots.

Madam hears the scandal
  With a wrathful frown,
Brings her tiny boot-heel
  With a vengeance down;
Up the street, indignant,
  Dashes with a swell—
Wag bawls " Muskrat!
  Know it by the smell."

Swimming down the sidewalk,
  Sweeping 'cross the street,
Head and hands in motion,
  Timing to the feet;
Right foot up and ready,
  Ere the left is down--
Bless me! what a bustle
  Coming through the town.

JOHN BRICK.

When first this cruel war broke out,
  John Brick was one of many,
Who vowed that for the cause they'd die,
  Or give up their last penny.
    But when the call
    For volunteers
Was spread throughout the nation,
    He was not found
    'Mong the renowned
Who fought for her salvation.

And when the conscript law was passed,
  A substitute he hired,
But 'twasn't long before that way
  Of keeping out expired.
    And having tried
    By other means,
In vain, to stay home longer,
    He joined a band,
    A home command,
(Thus making it much stronger.)

And **now they've got** him in, he seems
   Greatly exasperated,
That *every* citizen is not
   To be a soldier fated.
      He thinks that he
      A judge should be
    Of other people's matters;
      Throws out his thoughts,
      And his retorts,
    And of their business chatters.

John Brick is not the only one,
   Who in this way has acted;
He represents a numerous class,
   Who would all go distracted,
      Could they not meet
      Upon **the** street
    Some **one not in** the service,
      On whom to pass
      Their surplus gas,
    They would be very nervous.

I CANNOT BUY A WIFE.

You ask me, Charley, why I wear
   This troubled look of late,
If I lament some favorite, snatched
   By unrelenting fate?
I do not mourn some cherished friend
   Relieved of wretched life;
I'm sad because I lack the sum
   To buy a loving wife.

Once I believed that song could win
   A woman's tender heart,
I read that rocks and trees were moved
   By **music's** potent **art.**
The illusion fled, **and now I know,**
   With sorrow I must speak,
The ring of cash alone will bring
   The blush to Beauty's cheek.

'Tis true I have a "rich" papa,
  With lands, and mills, and pelf—
But he may wish—perhaps he may,
  To have a wife himself.
You know he'll need it all to buy
  A wife in his old age,
A young bird will not stay with old,
  But in a golden cage.

And, Charley, I was once a youth,
  And did not wish to wed;
But now I'm of another mind,
  When thirty years have sped;
Unsightly gray deforms my locks,
  The dentist plagues my life;
I feel, I feel it is high time,
  For me to get a wife.

Since, for the need of solid cash,
  My life must lonely be,
I wear of late this troubled look—
  Which, my old friend, you see.
A hut beside the wood—a house—
  A dog—a gun—a book—
These are the only comforts now
  For which I e'er shall look.

When you grow tired of city life,
  And masquerade and show,
Would seek awhile some silent cell—
  Where flowers and virtues grow.
Come, welcome to my hermitage,
  Nor hasten to depart—
Here find, that if I lack a wife,
  I yet possess a heart.

THE BLESSINKS OF RAININK.

How plesink 'tis to set inside,
  With somethink nice to rede,
And watch the glumy eleminks
  A doin' of its deeds.

The frightin'd wimmin run along,
  Skeert eeny most to deth—
Lor! how they hold their dresses up,
  And how I hold my breth.

The leaves all got their faces washed,
  As blessed torrinks fell;
How happy is the feller now
  Who's got an umberell.

An umberell's a excelent thing,
  When in the rain you're caught;
But when it stops a raininck,
  Why, it isn't good for nought.

The rain is a nuther excelent thing,
  It wets the country round,
And makes the beets and parsnips
  Go pokin' up the ground.

Lightnin's poorer stuff, and made
  Of bottles and of silk,
And thunder's only made to spile
  And sour the morning's milk.

PRESENT AND FUTURE.

Within the Mersey's docks of late
  There was a mighty bustle,
That all the way to London town,
  Attracted Johnny Russell.

The Iron-clads, the Iron-clads,
  Demons of sea **and** ocean,
With several Captain Semmes' **aboard,**
  Moved with stately motion.

Then Adams **said:** My noble **Lord,**
  With Abe you'll have **a** tussle,
Should those monsters get to sea!
  So look out, Johnny Russell!

Then John the Little, cried O! dear!
    Won't some good Briton's swearing
Do something for the Isle that holds
    The Rothschild and the Baring.

The little Bedford then assumed
    The constable's high calling,
He summoned witnesses himself
    To save his land a mauling.

For ah! he recks not future woe,
    Sure as the chair we sit on,
The South, will some day burly grow,
    And thrash the burly Briton.

SOMEBODY.

Somebody's courting somebody,
    Somewhere or other, to-night,
Somebody's whisp'ring to somebody,
Somebody's list'ning to somebody,
    Under this clear moonlight.

Near the bright river's flow,
Running so still and slow,
Talking so soft and low,
    She sits with somebody.

Pacing the ocean's shore,
Edged by the foaming roar,
Words, never breathed before,
    Sound sweet to somebody.

Under the maple-tree,
Deep though the shadow be,
Plain enough they can see—
    Bright eyes has somebody.

No one sits up to wait,
Though she is out so late—
All know she's at the gate
    Talking with somebody.

Tip-toe to parlor door—
Two shadows on the floor—
Moonlight reveals no more—
   Susy and somebody.

Two, sitting side by side,
Float with the ebbing tide.
"Thus, dearest, may we glide
   Through life," says somebody.

Somewhere, somebody
Makes love to somebody,
   To-night.

EPISTLE TO THE LADIES.

Ye Southern maids and ladies fair,
   Of whatsoe'er degree,
A moment stop—a moment spare—
   And listen unto me.

The summer's gone, the frosts have come,
   The winter draweth near,
And still they march, to fife and drum,—
   Our armies!—do you hear?

Give heed then to the yarn I spin,
   Who says that it is coarse?
At your fair feet I lay the sin,
   The thread of my discourse.

To speak of shoes, it boots not here,
   Our Q. M.'s, wise and good,
Give cotton calf-skins twice a year,
   With soles of cottonwood.

Shoeless we meet the well-shod foe,
   And bootless him despise;
Sockless we watch, with bleeding toe,
   And him sockdologize!

Perchance our powder giveth out;
  We fight them then with rocks,
With hungry craws we craw-fish not,—
  But, Miss, we miss the socks.

Few are the miseries that we lack,
  And comforts seldom come;
What have I in my haversack?
  And what have you at home?

Fair ladies, then, if nothing loth,
  Bring forth your spinning-wheels;
Knit not your brow,—but knit to clothe
  In bliss our blistered heels.

Do not *you* take amiss, **dear miss,**
  The burden of my yarn;
Alas! I know there's many *a lass!*
  That doesn't care a darn.

But you can aid us, if you will,
  And Heaven will surely bless,
And Foote will vote to foot a bill
  For succoring our distress.

For all the socks the maids have made,
  My thanks, for all the brave,
And honored be your pious trade,
  The soldiers sole to save.

MY GIRL IN THE CALICO DRESS.

A flag for your upper-ten girls,
  With their velvets, and satins, and laces,
Their diamonds, and rubies, and pearls,
  And their milliner figures and faces!
They may shine at a party or ball,
  Emblazon'd with half they possess,
But give me, in place of them all,
  My girl in the calico dress.

She is plump as a partridge, and fair
  As the rose in its earliest bloom;

Her teeth will with ivory compare,
  And her breath with the clover perfume;
Her step is as free and as light
  As the fawn, whom the hunters caress;
And her eyes are as soft and as bright—
  My girl in the calico dress.

Your dandies and foplings may sneer
  At her simple and modest attire;
But the charm she permits to appear
  Would set a whole iceberg on fire !
She can dance—but she never allows
  The hugging, the squeeze, the caress—
She is saving all these for her spouse—
  My girl with the calico dress.

She is cheerful, warm-hearted and true,
  And kind to her father and mother;
She studies how much she can do
  For her sweet little sister and brother.
If you want a companion for life,
  To comfort, enliven and bless,
She is just the right sort for a wife—
  My girl in the calico dress.

—————

POPE AND SULTAN.

The Pope lives glorious in the land
Ablution fees are e'er at hand;
He drinks the very best of wine,
I wish the Pope's estate were mine.

But no, he is a sorry wight;
He tasts not love's supreme delight
No maiden's arms to him are ope—
No, no, I would not be the Pope.

The Sultan lives in mighty state,
He has a palace wide and great;
With many a wife with pretty face;
I wish mine was the Sultan's place.

And yet I've pity on the man;
If he obeys his Alkoran
He cannot drink one drop of wine—
No, no, this were no choice of mine.

Alone with neither would I change,
Not for a moment's speedy range ;
Yet cheerfully would I agree
To bear by turns each dignity.

Therefore, sweet love, one kiss from thee,
For now the Sultan I will be ;
Now, brothers, fill with sparkling wine,
For now the Pope's estate is mine.

THE JOLLY BACHELOR.

I am a jolly bachelor,
  So hearty, hale and free,
What people wish to marry for,
  Is more than I can see ;
I would not be a married man
  For woman, wit or money,
Or the responsibilities
  That comes with matrimony.
    So now, young ladies,
      Oh ! don't you wait for me,
    For I'll be a bachelor
      So hearty, hale and free.

Once in my boyish days. I know,
  Of love I used to dream,
A certain pretty girl in shorts,
  An angel then did seem ;
She's married now—I saw her, but
  A single year ago—
Her foot was on the cradle, and
  Her hand was in the dough.

Here's John and Ned, and Charlie, too,
  Have knelt before the altar,
And carelessly have slipped their necks
  Into the marriage halter ;
For care and toil and curtain talk,
  Of life they've sold their lease,
And wives, you know, can never mend
  The breaches of their peace.

Oh, 'tis a sorry sight to see
  One strive a wife to win,

For, like the lilies of the vale,
  They neither toil nor spin;
With talk they break your peaceful rest
  And scold the livelong day,
And sometimes with your handsome friend
  They take themselves away.

You may have heard of Mrs. Lot,
  Who, for a woman's fault,
Was changed into a pillar of
  The best Turk's Island salt;
It saved her husband then, but now,
  We many a husband have
Whom, far beyond such remedy,
  No salt would ever save.

I knew a "nice young lady" once,
  As lovely as a saint,
Her cheeks were red as roses, though
  I rather think with paint;
She used to sing enchantingly,
  Was quiet as a kitten,
I popped the question to her, and
  For answer got the mitten.

She married Fitz Roy Flash, Esquire,
  A member of the bar,
He thought he'd got an angel, and
  She fancied him a star;
They quarreled—he forsook the law
  For whiskey, cards, and stout—
Poor Mrs. Flash makes bonnets now,
  And Fitz Roy Flash flashed out.

But I am happy all the time,
  No one to ask me when
I come home rather late at night,
  "My dear, where have you been?"
And when I seek my quiet bed,
  Untouched by care or strife,
I'd rather sink into the arms
  Of Morpheus than a wife.

AUNT JEMIMA'S PLASTER.

Aunt Jemima, she was old,
  But very kind and clever ;
She had a notion of her own
  That she would marry never.
She said that she would live in peace,
  And she would be her master;
She made her **living** day by day
  By selling of a plaster.
    Sheepskin and beeswax
    Make this awful plaster ;
  The more you try to take it off,
  The more it sticks the faster.

She had **a sister, very** tall,
  And if she'd kept on growing,
She might have been a giant now,
  In fact there is no knowing;
All of a sudden she became
  Of her own height the master,
And all because upon each foot
  Jemima put a plaster.
    Sheepskin and beeswax
    Make this awful plaster ;
  The more you try to take **it off**,
  The more it sticks the faster.

Her neighbor had a Thomas cat
  That eat like any **glutton** ,
It never caught a mouse or rat,
  But stole both milk and mutton ;
To keep it home **she** tried her best,
  But never could be its master,
Until **she** stuck it to **the** floor
  With Aunt Jemima's plaster.
    Sheepskin and beeswax
    Make this awful plaster ;
  The more you try **to take** it off,
  The more it sticks the faster.

Now if you have a dog or cat,
  A husband, wife, or **lover,**
That **you would** wish to keep at home,
  This plaster just discover ;
And if you wish to live in **peace,**
  Avoiding all disaster,

Take my advice, and try the strength
  Of Aunt Jemima's plaster;
    Sheepskin and beeswax
    Make this awful plaster;
  The more you try to take it off,
  The more it sticks the faster.

———

JOE BOWERS.

My name it is Joe Bowers,
  I have got a brother Ike;
I came from old Missouri,
  Yes, all the way from Pike—
I'll tell you why I left there,
  And how I came to roam,
And leave my poor old mamma
  So far away from **home**.

I used to love a gal there,
  Her name twas Sally Black;
I asked her if she would marry me,
  She said it was a whack;
Says she to me "Joe Bowers,
  Before we hitch for life,
You'd better buy a little house
  To keep your little wife."

Say I to her " my dearest Sally,
  Oh! Sally, for your sake,
I'll go to California,
  And try to raise a stake."
Says she to me " Joe Bowers,
  You are the very man,
So here's a kiss to seal the bargain,
  And she chucked a dozen in.

When I got to that country,
  I hadn't nary red,
I had such wolfish feelings,
  I wished myself most dead;
But then I thought of Sally,
  And it made such feelings get,
And whispered hopes to Bowers,
  I wish I had 'em yet.

At length I went to mining.
  Put in my biggest licks,
Came down upon the shiners
  Just like a thousand bricks ;
I worked both late and early,
  In sun, in rain, in snow,
I was **working** for my Sally dear,
  'T'was all the same to Joe.

At length I got **a letter,**
  . It was from my brother **Ike,** ·
It came from old Missouri,
  Yes, all the way from Pike ;
It brought the gol-darnest news
  That ever you did hear ;
My heart it is a bursting,
  So pray excuse this tear.
              (Tears fall fast.)

It said that Sally was false to **me,**
  And that her love had fled,
That Sally had married a butcher,
  And the butcher's hair **was** red.
And more than that **the letter said,**
  ('Tis enough to **make one** swear,)
That Sally had **got a baby,**
  And the baby **had** red hair.
              (Sensation.)

And now I have told you all
  About this very sad affair,
How Sally was married to **a** butcher,
  And **the** butcher had red hair.
But whether baby was a girl **or boy,**

  The letter never said,
It only said that the baby's hair
  Was rather inclined to be red.
              (**Great** sensation.)

BOLD SOGER BOY.

Oh **there's** not a trade that's **going,**
Worth showing, or knowing,
Like that from glory growing, `
  For a bowld soger boy !
Where right or left **we go,**

Sure you know, friend or foe,
Will have the hand or toe
    From the bowld soger boy!
There's not a town we marched thro'
But ladies looking arch thro'
The window panes, will sarce thro'
The ranks to find their joy,
While up the street, each girl you meet,
With look so sly, will cry, " My eye!
Oh isn't he a darling,
    The bowld soger boy."

But when we get the rout,
How they pout and they shout,
While to the right about
    Goes the bowld soger boy.
'Tis then the ladies fair,
In despair, tear their hair,
But the devil a one I care,
    Says the bowld soger boy!
For the world is all before us,
Where the landladies adore us,
And ne'er refuse to score us,
    But chalk us up with joy.
We taste her tap, we ter her cap,
" Oh that's the chap for me," says she,
" Oh isn't he a darling,
    The bowld soger boy."

Then come along with me,
Gramachree, and you'll see
How happy you will be
    With your bowld soger boy."
Faith if you are up to fun,
With a run, 'twill be done,
In the snapping of a gun,
    Says 'he bowld soger boy.
And 'tis then that without, scandal,
Myself will proudly dandle
    Of our mutual flame, my joy!
May his light shine as bright as mine,
Till in the line he'll blaze, and raise
The glory of his corps,
    Like a bowld soger boy.

SLAP—BY KLUBS.

Ho, gallants ! brim the beaker bowl,
  And click the festal glasses, oh !
The grape will shed its sapphire soul
  To eulogise the lasses, oh !
And when ye pledge the lip and curl
  Of loveliness and glory, oh !
Here's a bumper to the gallant girl
  That smote the dastard tory, oh !

CHORUS :

  A bumber, a thumper,
    To loveliness and glory, oh !
  Here's a bumper to the gallant girl
    That smote the dastard tory, oh !
Our boys are fighting East and West,
  But our women do not linger, oh !
For they take their diamonds from the breast,
  And their rubies from the finger, oh !
And they send their darlings to the van
  Of honor and of glory, oh !
And they've all the spirit of a man
  To smite a dastard tory, oh !

PETER GRAY.

I'll tell you of a nice young man,
Whose name was Peter Gray,
And the town that he was born in
Was Pensylva-ni-a.

CHORUS—Blow ye winds of morning,
         Blow ye winds I oh,
         Oh blow ye winds of morning,
         h blow ye winds I oh.

This Peter Gray did fall in love,
All with a nice young gurl,
The first two letters of her name,
Was Loo-egge-ian-na Querl.
   Chorus—Blow **ye** winds, &c.

Just as they were gwine to wed,
Her father did say no,
And quen-ci-cont-ly she was sent
Beyond the O-hi-o.
   Chorus—Blow ye winds, &c.

When Peter heard his love was lost,
He knew not what to say;
He'd half a mind to jump into
The Sus-que-han-i-a.
   Chorus—Blow ye winds, &c.

But he went traveling **to** the West,
For furs and other things,
And there was caught, and killed and drest
All by the In-gi-ins.
   Chorus—Blow ye winds, &c.

When Lo-egge-ian-na heard the news
She straightway went to bed,
And never did get up again
Until she di-i-ed.
   Chorus—Blow ye winds, &c

Ye **fathers** all a warning take,
Each **one** as has a gurl,
And think upon poor Peter Gray
And Loo-egge-ian-na Querl.
   Chorus—Blow ye winds, **&c.**

RATIO IN OMNIBUS.

Ho! all ye conscript Congressmen of this Confederation,
Deep learned in law, renowned in arms and wise in legislation,
Attend! I sing the "Ration Act"—a subject truly national—
The Ration Act—of all your acts the one that's most irrational.

Most potent, grave and reverend," why have you outlawed us?
At one fell blow, you've laid us low—incontinently *chawed* us;
Have made our bars and stars a theme for all the senseless scoffers,
     sirs;
Made toasting-forks of all our swords, and cooks of all our officers!

No one was heard complaining while you let us keep our niggers;
Content were we to buy our food at most enormous figures:
But now your cursed Ration Law has put them to the right about,
Our *niggers*, mind—the very things we first came out to fight
     about!

An officer must now ignore all ancient forms and fashions,
He cannot ask a friend to dine—'twould take a fortnight's rations;
They throw him meat—he bolts it raw—he lives like any cannibal,
Yet wears his only shirt as grand as Carthagenian Hannibal!

At early dawn he girds his loins, for marching—fighting—drilling;
His threadbare jacket lacks the warp—his stomach lacks the filling;
In faded gilt he strives to shine—Oh! do but note the pride of him,
With "chicken guts" upon his sleeves—and empty ones inside of
     him!

O, give us back our niggers, or we are, indeed, forsaken,
And issue them a little beef—'twill help to save your bacon;
"Beef! beef!" rare beef! (God bless the mark! 'tis rare enough
     we draw it, sirs,)
Although it be so lean and tough the devil couldn't chaw it, sirs!

The gay *Virginia* officer can still in plenty wallow,
Gets coffee, whisky, turtle soup—as much as he can swallow;
"Sugar in his'n" he always takes—draws army-gray to dress in,
And looks as neat, and smells as sweet, as a Catalonian jessamine!

Let Fame with trump-inverted sound our Western army's praises,
And when you mention "Rapidan," change ends and blow like
 blazes!
Even let her blow and burst her throat—and then she'll have to
 stop her lies;
But 'tis not fair that Lee should both the *praise* and *grub* monopo-
 lize!

O, Braxton Bragg! how can you stand this monstrous imposition?
This thrice invidious favoritism—this wholesale *abolition?*
Had I Jeff Davis' private ear, before I would allow it, sirs,
I'd set up such a roar he'd think 'twas *Meade* with all his howitzers!

Should e'er some future Dahlgren, with his friends besiege **our**
 Capital,
I'm sure we soldiers wouldn't think it any great mishap, at all;
We'd smuggle all the ladies out, the whisky and the President,
And give the devil a bill of sale of every other resident.

Since, then, 'tis from our *friends,* and not our foes, we need protec-
 tion;
When next the ballot-box comes round, we'll make a new selection;
Conscribe the fools—hang up the knaves—lop off the parasitical,
And Common Sense shall rise, a sun, upon the sky political!

"Sweet, oh sweet's de niggar's banjo hum."

DE NIGGER'S BANJO HUM.

'See darkies see, de sun sets fast,
Our pleasure time am cum at last,
Soon from de field to de house we'll come,
All to de banjo's cheerin' hum.
   Make haste, let us work
     Till ole sun's out ob sight,
  An' fold up de sheaves,
     Till de mornin' light.
Den round de house our heels we'll drum,
All to de banjo's cheerin' hum.
   Hum, hum, hum,
   De nigger's banjo hum,
    Sweet, oh sweet's de nigger's banjo hum,
   Hum, hum, hum, &c.

See now de light am dim an' dull,
An' night shines like de nigger's wool,
See how Sambo works his shin,
See how Cudjo's eye balls grin.
   Make haste, let us walk
     From our labor away,
  An' rest by a break down,
     Till broke ob de day.
All round de house de gals now come,
To hear de nigger's banjo hum,
   Hum, hum, hum,
   De nigger's banjo hum,
    Sweet, oh sweet's de nigger's banjo hum,
   Hum, hum, hum, &c.

GAILY THE CONGRESSMAN.

AIR.—*Gaily the Troubadour.*

Gaily the Congressman
  Dream'd of his skill—
How he extortioners
  Ever would kill;
Singing ye arrant knaves
  Quick now give o'er!
Robbers and renegades!
  Scourge of the poor!

Vainly the Congressman
  Dream'd that his bill
Funding old Treasury notes
  Extortion would kill;—
Discount is all the go
  Even on "fives,"
Robb'd is the laborer,
  Robb'd soldiers' wives!

Try again Congressman,.
  Head off the knaves,
Robbers and renegades,
  Slaves! Mammon's slaves!
Then may you gaily sing:
  Hither I come!
Constituents, constituents!
  Welcome me home!

AWAY TO DE 'BACCO FIELD.

Chorus.—Away to de 'bacco field,
  De sun am afore us,
We'll make de stalks now reel,
  And sing our jolly chorus.
    We'll poke a leaf
    Between our teef,
  Den chaw and cut away, boys;
    De 'bacco breeze
    Will make us sneeze,
  Like chickens in dry hay, boys.
    Away to de 'bacco, &c.

  Cut, cut de nigger plant,
    Dark as our own skin, boys;
Sing, sing de nigger's chaunt,
    Make de driver grin, boys.
      He'll curl his lip
      Throw down his whip,
    An' dance with us an hour.
      Den wid a blow
      To work he'll go,
    An' smile like a 'bacco flower.
        Away to de 'bacco, &c.

THE CAPTAIN.

As they marched through the town with their banners so gay,
I ran to the window to hear the band play;
I peeped thro' the blinds very cautiously then,
Lest the neighbors should say that I looked at the men
Oh! I heard the drums beat, and the music so sweet,
But my eyes at that moment had a much greater treat,
The troop was the finest that ever I did see,
And the Captain with his whiskers took a sly glance at me.

When we met at the ball, I, of course, thought 'twas right
To pretend that we never had met till that night;
But he knew me at once, I perceived by his glance,
And I looked down and blushed when he asked me to dance.

Oh; he sat by my arm at the end of the set,
And the sweet words he spoke I never can forget;
For my heart was enlisted, and could not get free,
As the Captain with his whiskers took a sly glance at me.

But he marched from the town, and I see him no more,
Yet I think of him oft, and the whiskers he wore;
I dream all the night and I talk all the day
Of the love of a Captain who went far away.
I remember with superabundant delight
When we met in the street, and we danced all the night,
And keep in my mind how my heart jumped with glee
As the Captain with the whiskers took a sly glance at me.

But there's hope, for a friend, just ten minutes ago,
Said the Captain's returned from the war, and I know
He'll be searching for me with considerable zest,
And when I'm found—ah! you know all the rest.
Perhaps he is here—let me look round the house—
Keep still every one of you, still as a mouse,
For if the dear creature is here, he will be
With his whiskers a taking sly glances at me.

THE LIGHT RICHMOND BRIGADE.

At morn and at even,
Thick as stars in high heaven,
  Their uniform satin, and silk, and brocade;
March out in full feather,
In soft winter weather,
  The sweetest of creatures, the Richmond Brigade.

Their lips are like roses,
Blushing daylight discloses,
  Their teeth are like pearls that in Aiden are made:
There's Venus and Juno,
All the goddesses, you know,
  That fill up the ranks of the Richmond Brigade.

'Tis strange how each beauty
Performeth her duty,
  When this phalanx of satin is out on parade;
"Forward, march! eyes to right, girls!
On the foe take good sight, girls!"
  Is heard in the ranks of the Richmond Brigade.

As a thousand bright lances
Shoot the fire of their glances,
   Doing damage enough in sunshine and **shade**;
When the witches all rout you,
How they laugh and they shout, too:
" Rush **to** arms ! Hurrah ! **for** the Richmond Brigade."

Then a health to the lasses !
Ho ! fill up your glasses!
   With something teetotaler Neptune ne'er made ;
And again, and again, boys,
To the daylight and night joys,
   To be found in the ranks of the Richmond Brigade !

—◆—

DE OLD ROAST POSSUM.

PARODY ON " THE OLD ARM CHAIR."

Oh ! I lub it, I lub it, dat old roast possum,
Wid de trimmins ob de coon, and some greens where I cotch him,
'Tis a berry luscious dish when de appetite am good,
And de Ingin pudding wid it, aen it am de best ob food ;
'Tis den I long to sit by de table wid my lub,
And watch de little niggers while dey are eatin ob de grub,
Oh, 'tis den we are so happy when we all set a watching,
As de last piece go from de bones ob de possum.

And **when we see** de last ob de possum's remains,
Old Dinah moves de dishes wid de greatest ob pains,
And de time de room is cleared de niggers begin to come
When dey all prepare to dance and to hab a little fun ;
Den old Cæsar wid his banjo goes and takes his place,
And plays up dem old tunes, suited to de nigger's taste,
Den we dance away **till** midnight, till **de** owls begin to screech,
And de bullfrogs **and de** crickets am **woke up** from dar sleep.
2*

" Come out of them ere boots."

THE FANCY CONSCRIPT.

It is of a gay young conscript a story I will tell,
Of the trials that he met with, and all that him befell ;
He kept from volunteering, for a substitute had he,
And many were his dodges, to keep clear of General Lee.

This North Carolina conscript was a very nice young man,
But this " fighting for his country" was not our hero's plan ;
He left the good old goober State, the officers to flee,—
Stumbled over a Conscript Guard who put him in Camp Lee.

To make the best of a bad thing, as always was his way,
And as he could not help it, he made up his mind to stay ;
Pens, ink and paper he did get, and thus wrote to his dad :
" I am bound to be a soldier, the thing is not so bad.

So send me on some ' Confeds,' of clothes I shall want two suits
And with the other little things, a pair of great big boots,

A gallon of good brandy, and a peck of goober peas,
I'll fight for glorious liberty, and sail through bloody seas."

It was not very long before a great big box did come
All the way from Carolina, this fancy conscript's home;
And soon was dressed our hero, in one of his gray suits,
With both his legs quite hid away in two enormous boots.

With his pockets full of goobers, and plenty ready cash,
He started off to see the girls, and cut a jolly dash;
But soon his troubles did begin, no furlough did he get—
French leave he took, and off he went, but soon got in a pet.

Soon the boys began to eye him, and presently did shout:
"Come out of them ere boots, for I can see your ugly snout."
No matter where he turned to go, he could not get away,
The young Confeds were after him and bound to have their say.

This was more than he could stand, so he started on a run,
But passing round a corner he was brought to by a gun;
" Your pass, your pass," the guard did cry, " whither do you
        flee ?"
" I came to see the town," quoth he, " and I'm running to Camp
        Lee."

" Your pass, I say : that may be so, but I must do my duty;
You look just like a thief, and your legs are in the booty ;
I think that fancy suit of gray, without a bit of lace,
You've taken from some officer, I see it in your face."

Poor Conscript knew not what to say, so jumped into the guard,
And soon a crowd was gathered round—the blows were thick and
        hard,
Our hero soon found out, he had made another blunder,
For now he is cracking goobers in the famous Castle Thunder.

OUR BABY.

My dear wife and I have a sweet little baby,
    As fat as a coon in the fall;
And in mischief, fun, frolic, or whate'er it may be
    He's the leader of *Infantry* all.

In consideration
Of his qualification,
I'm in contemplation
  Of making a bet,
That no father and mother,
On this cont'nent or tother,
Can produce such another
  As our little pet.

He's a year old to-day, and I'll venture to wager
  In fall, winter, summer, or spring,
You never saw yearling could compare with our " Major,"
  The baby whose praises I sing.
      He's just in condition
      To seek competition,
      And he's on exhibition
        At noon, night and morn,
      And if father or mother,
      Or sister or brother,
      Can produce such another,
        We'll " own up the corn."

LAMENT OF THE CAPTURED RAIDERS.

Air.—" Last rose of summer."

Kilpatrick! Kilpatrick!
  You promised our crew
Should burn and should pillage
  All Richmond with you;
We had only to loosen
  Our boys on Belle Isle,
And hang the big Rebels,
  Then sit down " to smile."

We dashed to the breastworks,
  All scorning a muss,
'Stead of *rifling* the " milish,"
  " Milish" *rifled* us!

We thought they'd skeddadle,
  'Ere think of their biers,
But the "milish" are captors,—
  Alas! we are theirs!

We're the last of the raiders
  Left horseless, alone,
All our jolly companions
  Are scattered and gone;
Sad "change this of *base*"
  For a-*base*-ment within
The walls of the Libby,
  Without friends or " tin !"

PIPES AND CIGARS.

Aır.—*Gentle Zitella.*

Fragrant Havana!
  Sweet, social star!
Bundle of manna!
  Matchless cigar!
Ere I surrender
  The taste of thy tips,
Rosa Matilda
  May pass with her lips!

Ike Marvel, hither,
  Come quick to me;
With thy wrath wither
  All foes of thee!
Alone in the corner
  I see thee now—
Feet on the fender,
  Peace on thy brow;

Smoke curling grandly
  Up from thy mouth,
Looking so blandly,
  Like saint of the South;
While on thy vision
  Bright dreams come fast;
Dreams of Elysian,
  Dreams of the past.

See the old people,
  How snugly they sit,
Straight as a steeple,
  Pipes all well lit ;
Laughing and smiling,
  Angelic, not gruff ;
Hours beguiling,
  With each pleasant puff.

Sweethearts ! no lover
  Can ever slight thee,
If spiral wreaths hover
  As now over me !
Housewives ! remember
  The sedative power,
That makes chill December
  Like May's rosy hour.

————◆————

TRUE TO HIS NAME.

In ancient days, Jehovah said,
  In voice both sweet and calm :
Be Abram's name forever changed
  To that of Abraham.

'Twas then decreed, his progeny
  Should occupy high stations,
For Abraham, in Hebrew, means
  "Father of many nations."

In Yankeeland, an Abraham,
  With speeches wise nor witty,
Went down to his Jerusalem,
  The famous Federal city.

True to his name, this Abraham will,
  So changed are his relations,
Instead of one great nation, be
  Father of many nations !

ELZEY'S PROCLAMATION.

AIR.—*Teddy the Tyler.*

From headquarters, the other night,
A courier came, with all his might,
To say that Elzey was in for a fight,
    And must have some Marylanders.
So, a proclamation did appear.
In newspapers, both far and near,
That the boys did not like, it was very clear,
And for Maryland some shed a tear.
    So like a bombshell did it fall,
    That over the boys it threw a pall;
    They did not know what to do at all
        With Elzey's proclamation.

" What shall we do ?" they all did say ;
" I'm afraid the South has had its day,
And soon there'll be the devil to pay
    Among us Marylanders.
The substitute dodge is all played out,
Our ' games' are done without a doubt ;
If they catch us, we will get the knout ;
What shall we do ?" they all did shout.
    So like a, &c.

To ruin he's brought us near the brink,
We're " aliens" all, if we dare to shrink ;
They've shut down even on a drink
    By us poor Marylanders.
My Maryland, I love thy shore—
Ah! would I were in Baltimore,
I'd ne'er forsake thy bounteous store,
But cling to thee for ever more,
    So like a, &c.

No use to cry, the milk is spilled ;
My pockets are lined, stomach's been filled .
I've had a good time, others got killed
    To save us Marylanders.

So Maryland, I'm for the fight,
To the front, and on Elzey's right,
We'll give the Yanks the bayonet bright,
Till every foe is out of sight.
      So, like a bombshell we will fall
      And over the Yankees throw a pall;
      Responding with vigor to the call
         Of Elzey's proclamation.

THE MUSICAL CAT.

The cat came out from under the barn,
With a fiddle-stick under his arm,
And all the tune that he could play,
Was "over the hills and far away."
Over the hills, and a great way off,
Where 'possums die of the whooping cough!
Over the hills, and a great way off,
Where 'possums die of the whooping cough!—
[This was the last ever heard of the *mew*-sical cat.]

A CONSCRIPT'S TROUBLES.

Come all ye jolly volunteers
  Who have been into the wars,
I will tell you my sad story,
  And how made a son of Mars.

My age is twenty-five or more,
  And I never liked to fight;
So when this cruel war began
  I just kept out of sight.

The conscript guard they dodged about,
  And I tried to do the same;
They wanted to put me in the front,
  Do you think I was to blame?

At last one day a fellow asked
   Me, if I had got a pass;
Says I, why don't you see I have,
   I belong to the " Second Class."

I pulled the *needful* out to give
   This old, ugly conscript guard ;
No, no, says he, " Confeds" won't do,
   You'll have to come the " hard."

I'll **tell** you what I'll do, says I,
   If you will not me pursue,
I will come back here to-morrow
   And bring you the " new issue."

He placed his thumb against his nose
   In a very vulgar way,
And said, " Do you take me for a fool ?
   With me you have to stay."

So up the street **we** both did go,
   Says I, Let's have **a** smoke ;
Not now, says he, I have no time,
   You can *treat* with Captain Coke.

I always like to **treat** a friend,
   And with friends to pass a joke ;
Some men I do not like at all—
   I don't like Captain Coke.

But 'twas no use, I had to go,
   I saw no chance to flee :
It **was** not many **hours** before
   They'd sent me to Camp Lee.

But now I have got a furlough,
   And am just come down to tell
All you who have not volunteered
   You had better be in ——
                [*Exeunt*]

[*Encore.*]

Now since you've call'd me out again,
 I'll tell you what I skipp'd,
Old soldiers, do not be too hard
 On this Camp Lee conscript.

And when you get me in the field,
 Tho' I should make a blunder,
Don't cry, " Conscript, run away !"—
 I don't like Castle Thunder.

And you young men who still keep out,
 By many an artful blunder,
Don't laugh at me, you'll yet be caught
 By Coke or General Winder.

PATRIOTIC AND SENTIMENTAL SONGS.

MARYLAND, MY MARYLA

What the Conscript Officers sung while after Maryland Papers.

Conscribers' **heels** are at thy door,
    Maryland, my Maryland!
With bayonets behind, before,
    Maryland, my Maryland!
They call on all from Baltimore,
Who, snugly on Virginia's shore,
Have failed to raise the cry of yore:
    Maryland, my Maryland!

You will not cower in the dust,
    Maryland, my Maryland!
Too long your swords have known the rust,
    Maryland, my Maryland!
Bomb proof no more, you know your trust,
For come you can and come you must,
Out with your swords and give a thrust,
    Maryland, my Maryland!

Ho! rush fast to the battle plain,
    Maryland, my Maryland!
Don't mind the thick **and** leaden rain!
    Maryland, my Maryland!
Hark! Johnson calls, and Marshal Kane
"What care **our** boys for thousands slain?
Should they get killed, they'll live again,
    Maryland, **my** Maryland!

And when this cruel war is o'er,
   Maryland, my Maryland!
Some may again see Baltimore,
   Maryland, my Maryland!
Though rather late, you can tell o'er,
How each strong sword was dipp'd in gore
From Bethel Fort to Grand Ecore,
   Maryland, my Maryland!

HURRAH, MY BRAVE BOYS.

Come, Southrons, and bare to the glorious strife,
  Your hearts without heaving a sigh:
Our cause it is just, and far dearer than life,
  We will conquer our foes, or we'll die.
     Then hurrah, my brave boys, with rifle in hand,
     We'll defend every home in our dear native land.

Loved ones that are ours, we'll willingly trust
  To the strong arms and hearts of the brave;
No Yankee can trample our forefather's dust—
  They would rise with a frown from the grave.
    Then hurrah, &c.

In no home of the South can a spoiler abide,
  No vandal can taste of its charms;
Shall a Yankee Zouave insult at our side
  The ones we've embraced in our arms?
    Then hurrah, &c.

The Yankees in arms may outnumber our braves,
  But when dead, other brave hearts and true,
Our wives, sisters and sweethearts will never be slaves,
  They will rush to the fight, and renew.
    Then hurrah, &c.

To arms, ye brave Southrons, to arms, be the cry,
  Every inch of our soil to defend,
Our loved ones we'll save, or else we will die,
  And our rifles to others extend.
    Then hurrah, &c.

Can a tyrant enslave such bold hearts as are here?
Or subdue us with sword or with flame?
Can the hordes of the North make one heart quake with fear,
While we trust in our battle God's name?
Then hurrah, &c.

BRIGHTLY THE SOUTHERN CROSS IS GLEAMING.

. Air—"Rally round the flag."

|Written for, and sung by the "Rebelonians," Johnson's **Island** Prison, April, 1864.|

With the fierce, terrific roar
Of five hundred guns or more,
A doom over Sumter long was seeming,
But they gave up in despair,
For our Beauregard was there,
And brightly the Southern Cross was gleaming!
　　Shoulder to shoulder, with hearts firm and true,
　　We never can be conquered by an Abolition crew,
　　　　For wherever is seen
　　　　Our bayonet's sheen,
　　Brightly the Southern Cross is gleaming!

When Gilmore's mongrel horde
Into Florida was poured,
Fondly of triumph he was dreaming,
But his columns backward reeled
From Olustee's bloody field
Where brightly the Southern Cross was gleaming!
　　Shoulder to shoulder, &c.

The miscreant Dahlgren thought,
As he led his base cohort,
That with blood the streets of Richmond would be streaming,
But he tasted Southern lead,
While above his gory head
Brightly the Southern Cross was gleaming!
　　Shoulder to shoulder, &c.

Brave Forrest, once again,
With his gallant mounted men,

Has filled the Yankee heart with terror teeming;
  At Fort Pillow he has paid
  The full price of Sherman's raid,
And brightly the Southern Cross is gleaming !
    Shoulder to shoulder, &c.

  Since Banks quit keeping store
  For Stonewall Jackson's corps,
Louisiana's ruin he's been scheming,
  But his star, at Grand Ecore,
  Has set to rise no more,
And brightly the Southern Cross is gleaming !
    Shoulder to shoulder, &c.

  With Lee in the East,
  And Johnson in the West,
Brightly the star of hope is beaming !
  Our success in '64
  Will end a glorious war—
Proudly the Southern Cross is gleaming !
    Shoulder to shoulder, &c.

THE GRAVE OF WASHINGTON.

Disturb not his slumbers, let Washington sleep
'Neath the boughs of the willow that over him weep ;
His arm is unnerved, but his deeds remain bright,
As the stars in the dark vaulted heaven at night
O ! wake not the hero, his battles are o'er,
Let him rest undisturbed on Potomac's fair shore—
On the river's green border so flowery drest,
With the hearts he loved fondly, let Washington rest.

Awake not his slumbers, tread lightly around,
'Tis the grave of the Freeman, 'tis Liberty's mound,
Thy name is immortal, our freedom ye won,
Brave sire of Columbia, our own Washington.
O ! wake not the hero, his battles are o'er,
Let him rest, calmly rest, on his dear native shore,
While the stars and the bars of our country shall wave,
O'er the land that can boast of a Washington's grave.

PLUCK WILL WIN.

True soldier pluck the wide world o'er
   Will win in peace or war;
When loud the flashing cannon's roar,
   When trills the light guitar.
Be't for a kiss, with maid or wife,
   For life's blood, with the foe,
The soldier's eager for the strife,—
   For **pluck** will win, you know,
     Hurrah!
For pluck will win, you know.

Where sweeps the dance in giddy whirl,
   And bright **eyes** flash with joy,
The arm enclasps the laughing girl,
   And hand with hand may toy;
Who sues too long ne'er wins a kiss—
   The soldier woos not so,
But dashes boldly on to bliss,
   For pluck will win, you know,
     Hurrah!
   For pluck will win, you know

For when on sultry summer's day,
   The march is far and fast,
The gallant charger's strength gives way,
   He sinks and falls at last;
The soldier keeps his courage up,
   And sings, re-too-ral loo;
For he will neither taunt nor drop,
   Sheer pluck will take him through,
     Hurrah!
   Sheer pluck will take him through.

And where proud banners flaunt the **gale**,
   And hostile columns clash,
And far and near, o'er hill and dale,
   The iron thunders crash;
Far flashing steel from out **the strife**
   Sends forth its glittering ray;
There, man to man, or life to life,
   True pluck will win the day,
     Hurrah!
   True pluck will win the day.

And should my mortal hour be nigh,
  I'm ready, prompt at hand;
'Tis not for sordid gold I die,
  But for my fatherland!
I've done my duty like a man,
  And sealed it with my blood!
So live—so die—be that your plan,
  And pluck will make it good,
      Hurrah!
  And pluck will make it good!

SEVENTY-SIX AND SIXTY-ONE.

Ye spirits of the glorious dead!
  Ye watchers in the sky!
Who sought the patriot's crimson bed
  With holy trust and high—
Come lend your inspiration now,
  Come fire each Southern son,
Who nobly fights for freemen's rights,
  And shouts for sixty-one.

Come teach them how on hill, in glade,
  Quick leaping from your side,
The lightning flash of sabres made
  A red and flowing tide;
How well ye fought, how bravely fell,
  Beneath our burning sun,
And let the lyre, in strains of fire,
  So speak of sixty-one.

There's many a grave in all the land,
  And many a crucifix,
Which tells how some heroic band
  Stood firm in seventy-six—
Ye heroes of the deathless past,
  Your glorious race is run,
But from your dust springs freemen's trust,
  And blows for sixty-one.

We build our altars where you lie
  On many a verdant sod,
With sabres pointing to the sky
  And sanctified of God—
The smoke shall rise from every pile,
  Till Freedom's fight is done,
And every mouth throughout the South,
  Shall shout for sixty-one.

THE BELLE OF LOUISIANA.

Go search beside the Rhine, the **Rhone**,
  Arno and Guadalquiver!
In many a fair and verdur'd land,
  By many a stately river;
Go look for eyes all starry bright,
  In blonde, or dusk Sultana,
But leave for me her orbs of light—
  The Belle of Louisiana!

Not Juno in her maiden bloom,
  Not Venus with her cestus,
Not all the gods Olympus sent
  To dazzle and invest us,—
Not all the lips the Prophet saw
  Fed with celestial manna,
Can tempt me from my light, my love—
  The Belle of Louisiana!

As a folded rose her lips unclose,
  And honied tones beset us,
Soft as the murmur of the bees
  Of Hybla and Hymettus;
Ho! wine of Samia **for** the fair
  From Oman's **sea to** Banna,
And bumpers to the Queen of Love—
  The Belle of Louisiana! ·

WE'LL DIE OR YET BE FREE!

Southrons, march to scenes of glory!
Glit'ring bayonets tell the story
To hireling hosts on battle field-gory,
　　　We'll die or yet be free!

See, the vandal Butler is nigh,
On our Capital rests his eye,
"At them boys!" and raise the cry,
　　　We'll die or yet be free!

"On to Richmond!" still they cry,
Answer Southrons, " Do or die!"
Let our shouts resound on high,
　　　We'll die or yet be free!

Hark! the booming cannon sounds,
Lingering death and gaping wounds
Is dealt unto the Yankee hounds,
　　　We'll die or yet be free!

THE PILOT.

Oh, Pilot! 'tis a fearful night,
　There's danger on the deep,
I'll come and pace the deck with thee,
　I do not dare to sleep.
Go down! the sailor cried, go down,
　This is no place for thee;
Fear not! but trust in Providence,
　Wherever thou may'st be.

Ah! Pilot, dangers often met,
　We all are apt to slight,
And thou hast known these raging waves
But to subdue their might.
It is not apathy, he cried,
　That gives this strength to me,
Fear not! but trust in Providence,
　Wherever thou may'st be.

On such a night, the sea enguiph'd
　My father's lifeless form
My only brother's boat went down,
　In just so wild a storm;

And such perhaps may be my fate,—
  But still I say to thee,
Fear not! but trust in Providence,
  Wherever thou may'st be.

FOR HOME AND LIBERTY.

Air—When the Trump of Fame.

Sons of the free unite,
  And nobly heart and hand,
Against oppression's might,
  Defend your native land ;
Hark ! Freedom's Genius loud,
  Now calls in stirring cries,
And echo from the cloud,
  Elate replies.

Light the glorious fires,
  That brightly burnt of yore,
When our undaunted sires
  Hushed the Lion's roar;
Swear that the right they gave
  You'll cherish pure and free,
And strike by land and wave
  For Home and Liberty !

Hark ! loud through the air,
  Rings battle's gory hour,
Confederate daughters fair,
  With woman's magic power,
The souls of freemen cheer,
  With glowing eyes of fire,
And without a tear,
  All hearts inspire!

Their woven flags wave high,
  With each gallant hand,
Amid their farewell cry,
  " Go strike for Freedom's land ;'
Then as from angel lips,
  Roll forth their blessings free;
'Till heaven joins the cry,
  For Home and Liberty !

THE MAIDS OF THE SOUTH.

A truce to your wars
    And your armor-clad Mars!
Let us sing to the lips we adore,
    So pulpy and red,
    Such a fragrance they shed,
'Twould craze either Schiller or Moore!

    Ho! high lift ye up
    The wine-crested cup,
To the stars of the bachelor's skies!
    To the maids of the South,
    With the musical mouth,
And their brilliantly beaming black eyes!

    Once again! and again!
    To the bottom we drain
The cup to the lips we adore;
    To the eyes and the lips
    Of the maids who eclipse
The sweethearts of Schiller and Moore!

WHEN THIS CRUEL WAR IS OVER.

Dearest one, do you remember
    When we last did meet?
When you told me how you loved me,
    Kneeling at my feet?
Oh! how proud you stood before me
    In your suit of grey,
When you vowed from me and country
    Ne'er to go astray!

Chorus.

    Weeping, sad and lonely,
        Sighs and tears how vain!
    When this cruel war is over,
        Praying then to meet again.

When the summer breeze is sighing,
  Mournfully along,
Or when autumn leaves are falling,
  Sadly breathes the song.
Oft in dreams I see you lying
  On the battle plain,
Lonely, wounded, even dying,
  Calling, but in vain.
          Chorus.

If amid the din of battle,
  Nobly you should fall,
Far away from those who love you,
  None to hear your call,
Who would whisper words of comfort ?
  Who would soothe your pain ?
Ah ! the many cruel fancies
  Ever in my brain !
          Chorus.

But our country called you, loved one,
  Angels guide your way !
While our Southern boys are fighting,
  We can only pray.
When you strike for God and freedom,
  Let all nations see
How you love our Southern banner,
  Emblem of the free !
          Chorus.

SONG FOR THE TIMES.

The flag that our fathers fought under,
  Is soiled by tyranny's hand ;
Then adieu, to the banner once cherished,
  Since borne by a treacherous band.
Up ! up with fair liberty's standard,
  (Our cause is of Justice and Right,)
The stars that now spangle her azure,
  Old Time should but render more bright.

The legacy that Washington left us,
  Of freedom, we'll cherish for aye;
No ensign of tyranny o'er us,
  No despot his sceptre shall sway.
If we die, we will conquer in dying,
  Our cry at the death-cannon's mouth
Be, "the flag of this Union forever
  The star-spangled flag of the South."

Chorus.

O! the star-spangled flag of the South,
The dear Union flag of the South,
  The flag of our Union forever!
The star-spangled flag of the South!

DON'T GIVE UP THE SHIP.

A braver motto ne'er was learned,
  From chieftain's dying lips:
"Oh, don't give up the ship, my boys,
  Oh, don't give up the ship!"
Go, nail your colors to the mast,
  And don't give up the ship!

Chorus.

We won't give up the ship,
We'll ne'er give up the ship,
Whilst Heaven protects the right my boys,
We won't give up the ship!

Mayhap, in many a roaring gale,
  We'll see her creen and dip;
But never night so grim and fierce,
  That we'll give up the ship,
We'll reach the port all right at last,
  And anchor our good ship

Chorus.

Thro' flame and smoke our streamer flies,
  The ensign of the brave;
And ne'er a barque more taut and trim,
  Hath gemmed the bounding wave.

Who says, 'Give up **the** ship!' my boys?
  Give up this noble ship?
Too much of patriot pride have we—
  We won't give up the ship!

Chorus.

Our pilot standing on the prow,
  With highest hopes elate,
Is strengthened by a mighty hand,
  To guide **our** ship **of** State.
We'll **reach the** port **secure** at **last,**
  However rough the trip;
Whilst Heaven protects the right my boys.
  We won't give up the ship.

Chorus.

THE YOUNG INDIAN **MAID.**

There came a nymph dancing,
  Gracefully, gracefully,
Her eye was light glancing
  Like the blue sea.
And while all this gladness
  Around her steps hung,
Such sweet notes of sadness
  Her gentle lips sung,
That ne'er while I live,
  From my memory shall fade,
The song of the look
  Of **that young** Indian maid.

Her zone of bells ringing,
  Cheerily, cheerily,
Chimed to her singing,
  Light echoes of glee.
But in vain did she borrow
  Of mirth the gay tone,
Her voice **spoke** of **sorrow,**
  And sorrow alone.
Nor e'er while I live
  From my memory shall fade,
The song or the look
  Of that young Indian maid.

THE MARCH.

Tramp, tramp, tramp, tramp,
  Go the Southern braves to battle,
How they shine, each gleaming line!
  Flashing sabres! how they rattle!
Every lip is now compressed,
  Every heart now yearns for glory,
Every eye with patriot fire
  Burns for battle fierce and gory!

Tramp, tramp, tramp, tramp,
  Death is in each hidden sabre.
Reaper of the fields of time,
  Look ye for a giant's labor!
How sublime! when patriots feel
  All the strength of self-reliance,
Marching on to meet the foe
  With a stern and grim defiance.

See how proudly floats our flag!
  White! our cause is pure and grand, man,
Red! a living tide shall flow
  From every foe now in the land, man,
Blue! aye, heaven's stars are there!
  Sparkling in their azure beauty
Tramp, tramp, tramp, tramp!
  . Go the messengers of duty!

VIRGINIA AND HER DEFENDERS.

Air—" Carolina, Carolina."

Virginia! Virginia! your children of glory
Are wedded forever to historic story;
They rushed to the field, and the cannon's loud rattle,
Showed the insolent foe how the free can do battle
  Huzza! huzza! for gallant Virginia,
  Huzza! huzza! for the brave and the free!
                     [Repeat

From city and village, from hill and from valley,
Virginia! Virginia, your champions rally,
As stars in the heavens, your sons are in motion.
Resistless are they as the waves of the ocean.
  Huzza! huzza! for gallant Virginia,
  Huzza! huzza! for the brave and the free!

How proudly each father, defying aggression,
Gives his son to the leaders who scorn all concession '
And each mother, Virginia, her brave child caressing,
Sends him out to the battle with God's and her blessing.
    . Huzza ! huzza' for gallant Virginia !
      Huzza**!** **huzza!** for the **brave** and the free !

Virginia ! Virginia' in the cannon's loud rattle,
Carolina and Georgia's by your side in the battle ;
Texas. Mississippi, Alabama, Louisiana,
Swell proudly the anthem of victory's hosanna !
      Huzza ' huzza ! for your gallant defenders '
      Huzza **!** huzza ! for the brave and the free '

Virginia ! Virginia ! no foe can enslave her.
She fights for the freedom her forefathers gave her ;
With her sisters she'll conquer the tyrant invader,
Retaining the glory that Washington made her.
      Huzza ! Huzza ! our heroes forever '
      Huzza' Huzza! for the brave and the free!

BALLAD OF FORT SUMTER.

Fort Sumter! Fort Sumter ! thou art married to Fame,
For the green wreath of glory encircles thy name ;
Forever be honor to the good and the brave,
Who stood on thy ramparts to guard and to save.

'Twas the thirteenth of April in the year sixty-one,
When thy flag of Palmetto gleamed in the sun,
And thy daughters, Carolina, looked out from afar,
To see on Fort Moultrie the liberty star !

On the walls of Fort Sumter the Yankee flag flew,
The symbol of tyrants to me and to you,
For the despot had sworn in the depths of his soul,
That his banner should fly while the billows should roll

How we watched through the day and the gloom of the night
The flash of the guns in the terrible fight ;
How leaped our hearts at the last bursting shell,
When from Sumter the symbol of tyranny fell

'Twas the seventh of April in the year sixty three,
When the Yankees assaulted the fort of the free :
From the walls of old Sumter our flag was unfurled,
The pride of the South **and the** hope of the world

Again ! O! again through the perilous fight,
Thy daughters, Carolina, prayed long for the right,
The Yankee armada was scattered and scarred,
All honor to Rhett and the brave Beauregard !

STONEWALL JACKSON'S WAY.

Come, **stack arms, men!** pile on the rails,
  Stir up the camp fire bright,
No matter if the canteen fails,
  We'll make a roaring light.
Here Shenandoah brawls along,
There burly Blue Ridge echoes strong,
To swell the brigade's rousing song
  Of "Stonewall Jackson's way."

We see him now, **the** old slouched **hat**
  Cocked o'er **his** eyes askew,
The shrewd dry smile, the speech so pat,
  So calm, so blunt, so true.
The "Blue Light Elder" knows 'em **well,**
Says he, "**That's Banks, he's fond of shell,**
Lord save his soul! we'll give him"—well,
  That's "Stonewall Jackson's way."

Silence! ground arms, kneel all, **caps** off,
  Old Blue Light's going to pray:
Strangle the fool that dare's to scoff,
  Attention! it's **his** way.
Appealing from **his** native **sod,**
In *forma pauperis* **to** God:
"Lay bare thine arm, stretch forth thy rod,
  Amen!" That's "Stonewall's way."

He's in the saddle now. Fall **in!**
  Steady, the whole brigade!
Hill's at the ford cut off—we'll win
  His way out, ball **and** blade.
What matter if **our shoes** are **worn?**
What matter if **our feet are torn?**
"Quick step! we're with him before morn,"
  That's "Stonewall Jackson's way."

TRUST TO LUCK.

Trust to luck, trust to luck, and stare fate in the face,
Shure your heart will be aisy if it's in the right place,
Let the world wag awry, and your friends turn foes,
When your pockets are dry, and threadbare your clothes;

Should woman deceive you **when** you trusted her heart,
Ne'er sigh will relieve you, **but** add to the smart ;
Trust to luck, trust to luck, **and stare** fate in the face,
Shure the heart will be aisy **if it's in** the right place.

Trust to luck, trust to luck, and you'll never forget,
Bright morning will follow the darkest night yet ;
Let the wealthy look grand, and the proud pass you by
With the back of their fist and disdain in their eye,
Snap your fingers and smile, let them pass on their way,
And remember the while every dog has his day.
Trust to luck, trust to luck, and stare fate in the **face**,
Shure the heart will be aisy if **it's in** the right place.

PIRATE'S CHORUS.

Ever be happy and bright as thou art,
Pride of the pirate's heart,
Ever be happy and bright as thou art,
Pride of the pirate's heart.
Long be thy reign o'er land and main,
By the glave, by the chart,
Queen of the pirate's heart,
Queen, ever be happy and bright as thou art.
Pride of the pirate's heart, &c.

THE RIGHT ABOVE THE WRONG.

In other days our fathers' love was loyal, full and free,
For those they left behind them in the Island of the Sea ;
They fought the battles of King George and toasted him in song,
For then the Right kept proudly down the tyranny **of** Wrong.

But when the king's weak, willing slaves laid **tax** upon the tea,
The western men rose up and braved the Island **of** the Sea ;
And swore a fearful oath to God, those men of iron might,
That in the end the Wrong should die, and up should go the
    Right.

The king sent over hireling hosts, Briton, Hessian, Scot,
And swore in turn those western men when captured should be
    shot,

While Chatham spoke with earnest tongue against the hireling
    throng,
And mournful saw the Right go down, and place give to the
    Wrong.

But God was on the righteous side, and Gideon's sword was out,
With clash of steel, and rattling drum, and freemen's thunder-
    shout ;
And crimson torrents drenched the land through that long,
    stormy fight,
But in the end, hurrah! the Wrong was beaten by the Right!

And when again the foemen came from out the Northern Sea,
To desolate our smiling land and subjugate the free,
Our fathers rushed to drive them back with rifles keen and long,
And swore a mighty oath, the Right should subjugate the Wrong.

And while the world was looking on, the strife uncertain grew,
But soon aloft rose up our stars amid a field of blue ;
For Jackson fought on red Chalmette and won the glorious fight,
And then the Wrong went down, hurrah! and triumph crowned
        the Right!

The day has come again, when men who love the beauteous
        South,
To speak, if needs be, for the Right, though by the cannon's
    mouth ;
For foes accursed of God and man, with lying speech and song,
Would bind, imprison, hang the Right ; and deify the Wrong.

But canting knave of pen and sword, nor sanctimonious fool,
Shall never win this Southern land to cripple, bind and rule ;
We'll muster on each bloody plain thick as the stars of night,
And through the help of God, the Wrong shall perish by the
        Right!

NOW WITH GRIEF NO LONGER BENDING.

    . Now with grief no longer bending,
        Shall my heart neglected sigh ?
    No! like the lightning swiftly ending,
        Sorrow's clouds for ever fly !
                        . Now with grief, &c.

OUR FLAG.

Up! up with our banner! let Heaven's winds fan her,
  No staff from the forest a purer flag bore;
No stain of dishonor casts shadows upon her,
  Her folds to the sunshine like eagle's wings soar.

The homestead's bright fires, the graves of our sires,
  Dear flag, we commit to thy keeping to-day;
Our heart's every treasure, come sorrow or pleasure,
  All cluster and group 'neath thy genial sway.

Ay, if firm to our duty, this flag in her beauty,
  Shall spread out in triumph o'er mountain and wave;
And, sworn to defend her, ere foemen should rend her,
  We'll find 'neath her shadow a patriot's grave!

Then fling out our banner, let Heaven's winds fan her,
  Up! up to the sun, like an eagle her flight;
Haste, freemen, beneath her, with laurels we'll wreathe her,
  Success to her mission! and God speed the Right!

THE MOCKING BIRD.

I'm dreaming now of Allie, sweet Allie, sweet Allie,
      I'm dreaming now of Allie,
For the thought of her is one that never dies;
She is sleeping in the valley, the valley, the valley—
      She's sleeping in the valley,
And the mocking bird is singing where she lies;
         Listen to the mocking bird,
         Listen to the mocking bird,
To the mocking bird still singing o'er her grave;
         Listen to the mocking bird,
         Listen to the mocking bird,
Still singing where the weeping willows wave.

Ah! well I yet remember, remember, remember,
      Ah! well I yet remember,
When we gathered in the cotton side by side;
'Twas in the mild September, September, September,
      'Twas in the mild September,
And the mocking bird was singing far and wide;
         Listen to the mocking bird,
         Listen to the mocking bird,
The mocking bird still singing o'er her grave;
         Listen to the mocking bird,
         Listen to the mocking bird,
Still singing where the weeping willows wave.

When the charms of spring awaken, awaken, awaken,
      When the charms of spring awaken,
And the mocking bird is singing on the bough,
I feel like one forsaken, forsaken, forsaken,
      I feel like one forsaken,
Since my Allie is no longer with me now;
         Listen to the mocking bird,
         Listen to the mocking bird,
The mocking bird still singing o'er her grave;
         Listen to the mocking bird,
         Listen to the mocking bird,
Still singing where the weeping willows wave.

THE WHITE SQUALL.

The sea was bright and the bark rode well,
The breeze bore the tone of the vesper bell,
'Twas a gallant bark with crew as brave
As ever launch'd on the heaving wave,
She shone in the light of declining day,
And each sail was set and each heart was gay.

They near'd the land where in beauty smiles,
The sunny shore of the Grecian Isles,
All thought of home of that welcome dear,
Which soon should greet each wand'rer's ear,
And in fancy join'd the social throng,
In the festive dance and in the joyous song.

A white cloud glides through the azure sky
What means that wild despairing cry ?
Farewell the vision'd scenes of home,
That cry is help where no help can come,
For the white squall rides on the surging wave,
And the bark is gulph'd in an ocean's grave.

ALL'S WELL.

Deserted by the waning moon,
When skies proclaim night's cheerless noon,
On tower, or fort, or tented ground,
The sentry walks his lonely round,
And should a footstep haply stray
Where caution marks the guarded way,
"Who goes there? Stranger quickly tell !"
"A friend"—the word—"Good night—All's well !"

Or sailing on the midnight deep,
While weary messmates soundly sleep,
The careful watch patrols the deck,
To guard the ship from foe or wreck ;
And while his thoughts oft homeward veer,
Some well known voice salutes his ear,
"What cheer! oh, brother! quickly tell !"
"Above! below! Good night! All's well !"

THEY ONLY ARE FREE WHO DESERVE TO BE FREE

Air—Garb of Old Gaul.

Confederates arise, none but cowards would yield !
Seize the death-dealing sword and rush on to the field !
From the soil of our sires sweep the insolent foe,
Though their blood to the ocean in torrents shall flow !
(Chorus.)
Fling out our Southern banner in the thickest of the fight!
Strike, Cavaliers, for fatherland, for Liberty and Right !
Till every bar
And glittering star
Shall blaze in victory's light,
And the nation, like a giant, shall deride the tyrant's might

Our fathers once trod the same land which we tread ;
Our fathers, stout heroes to battle once led ;
The proud lesson taught us, remembered should be—
They only are free who deserve to be free !
Fling out, &c.

By the sun-brilliant land our fathers bequeathed ;
By the liberty won when their sabres they sheathed ;
By the wives of our bosoms, by the God that's on high !
By our homes and our altars, we'll conquer or die !
Fling out, &c.

The invader may pillage, may burn and destroy,
But the darkest of nights brings its mornings of joy,
If the lesson once taught us remembered shall be,
They only are free who deserve to be free.
Fling out, &c.

ROSALIE CLARE.

Where the blue limpid Rhone, to the deep rolling seas,
Flows fast as the swift-footed antelope flees ;
Where the vineyards are seen in the soft Provence clime
That taught the young troubadours music and rhyme ;
Where the heart is as light as the swift gliding feet,
And the lilies of Gallia are graceful and sweet :
The maidens are fair,
And their beauties are rare,
Yet none have the graces
Of Rosalie Clare.

By the side of the Arno, whose soft-swelling breast
Burns bright in the blaze of the God of the West ;
Where the envious stars from their mansions above,
Look down in the eyes of the Venus of Love ;
Where the raptures of song from the warm passions shoot,
And the voice of the virgin sounds sweet as the lute ;

The maidens are fair,
But they cannot **compare**
With the sweet, witching beauty
Of Rosalie Clare.

Where the waves of the Tagus glide silent along,
To the strains of the troubadour's love-swelling song ;
And moonlight **and music** and beauties galore,
Ope a heaven **of happiness** ne'er seen before,
Till the heart, like **a** billow, with wild passion **swells,**
And the eyes grow bewildered with dark-eyed gazelles—
Though **the** maidens are **fair,**
What craven shall dare
To match these bright damsels
With Rosalie Clare.

Ho! weave me a garland **of** sweet-smelling flowers !
Ho! deck me the brow of this young queen of ours !
Ho! high on the throne of the gentle and blest,
Let her beam like a star in yon Heaven of rest !
Ho! Knights of Hispania, Italia and France,
I throw down the gauntlet! come, break me a lance—
Thy maidens are fair,
And their graces are rare,
Yet none have the **beauty**
Of Rosalie Clare.

— — —

I LOVE BUT THEE.

If after all you still **do doubt and** fear me,
And **say** this heart to other ones has strayed,
Since I must swear then lovely doubter hear me,
By every dream **of** sorrow thou art mine ;
I only think and feel when **thou** art near me,
I love but **thee, I** love but thee.

By those bright eyes where light **is** ever playing,
Where moon light sleepeth upon beams alone,
Or by **those** cheeks whose fleeting blush discloses
Art thou too bright to bless this heart **of mine,**
Thou art only fit to dwell on Eden's roses,
I love but thee, I love but thee.

SOLDIER'S DREAM.

Our bugles sang truce, for the night cloud had lower'd,
  And the sentinel stars set their watch in the sky;
And thousands had sunk on the ground overpower'd,
  The weary to sleep, and the wounded to die.

When reposing that night on my pallet of straw,
  By the wolf-scaring faggot that guarded the slain,
At the dead of the night a sweet vision I saw,
  And thrice ere the morning I dreamt it again.

Methought from the battle fields dreadful array,
  Far I had roam'd on a desolate track;
'Twas autumn—and sunshine arose on the way,
  To the home of my father that welcom'd me back.

I flew to the pleasant fields traversed so oft
  In life's morning march when my bosom was young,
I heard my own mountain-goats bleating aloft,
  And knew the sweet strain that the corn-reapers sung.

Then pledg'd we the wine cup, and fondly I swore,
  From my home and my weeping friends never to part;
My little one's kiss'd me a thousand times o'er,
  And my wife sobb'd aloud in the fulness of heart.

Stay, stay with us—rest, thou art weary and worn,
  And fain was the war-broken soldier to stay;
But sorrow return'd with the dawning of morn,
  And the voice of my dreaming ear melted away.

THE SOLDIER'S TEAR.

Upon the hill he turned to take a last fond look,
Of the valley and the village church, and the cottage by the
      brook;
He listened to the sound so familiar to his ear,
And the soldier leant upon his sword, and wiped away a tear.

Beside that cottage porch a girl knelt on her knees,
She held aloof a snowy scarf which flutter'd in the breeze;
She breath'd a prayer he could not hear,
But he paused to bless her, as she knelt and wiped away a tear,

He ... and left the spot—oh! do not deem him weak,
... intless was the soldier's heart, tho' tears were on
   cheek;
... tch the foremost ranks in danger's dark career,
... re the hand most daring there has wiped away a tear.

VIVE L'AMOUR.

He who wears a regimental suit,
Oft is poor as some ... recruit,
          But what of that!
Girls will follow when they hear the drum,
To view the tassel and the waving plume,
          That deck his hat!
C ... he will ... ng when he's not on duty,
Smoke his cigar or flirt with some gay beauty.
   Oh, vive l'amour, cigars and cognac,
      Hurra, hurra, hurra, hurra! with these we'll bivouac

When we march into a country town,
Prudes may fly from us, and dames may frown,
          All that's absurd!
When we march away we leave behind
Prudes and dames that have been vastly kind—
          Pray ... me word!
Off, off we go and tell them we're on duty,
Smoke a cigar, and ... ek for ... new beauty
   Oh, vive l'amour, &c.

THE VOICE OF HER I LOVE.

How sweet at close of silent eve
   The harp's responsive sound
How sweet the ... that ... decay,
   And deeds of virtue crown!
How sweet to sit beneath a tree
   In some delightful grove,
But ah! more sweet, more soft to me,
   Is the voice of her I ...

OUR SOUTHERN BOYS.

The Southern blood is running fast
  In Southern veins to-night;
Our gallant boys on tented fields
  Are eager for the fight!
On many a hill, on many a plain,
  Rifle, sabre, knife,
In bright array, flash night and day
  For mother, sister, wife!
    Hurrah! for our Southern boys!
      The ladies should adore them!
    Hurrah! our flag above them flies,
      While Heaven watches o'er them!

Yet though our boys are gone to war,
  And left the dear ones here,
They need not heave a single sigh,
  Nor shed a single tear;
For generous souls and open hands
  Each soldier left behind him,
So let him fight with all his might,
  Our hearts know where to find him!
    Hurrah! for our Southern boys!
      The ladies should adore them!
    Hurrah! our flag above them flies,
      While Heaven watches o'er them!

O! near to us, and dear to us
  Is every darling treasure
That round the soldiers' fireside,
  Fills home with love and pleasure;
And while the dear ones absent be,
  In patriot ranks of glory,
We'll wear their image in our hearts,
  And wed their names to story!
    Hurrah! for our Southern boys!
      The ladies should adore them!
    Hurrah! our flag above them flies,
      And Heaven watches o'er them!

www.ingramcontent.com/pod-product-compliance
Lightning Source LLC
Chambersburg PA
CBHW030021030726
47499CB00008B/3069